THIS BOOK BELONGS TO:

.....................................................

Written by Rosie Greening.
Illustrated by Nadine Wickenden.

# Little Ted's Big Heart

Rosie Greening • Nadine Wickenden

make
believe
ideas

In a **beautiful** forest
with trees everywhere,
there lived the most **friendly**
and **kind-hearted** bear.

Each day, Little Ted scampered off to have fun, and play with his **friends** in the warm summer **sun.**

So **one** evening, young Ted tried to **think** of a way to **show** all his friends that he **loved** them each day.

"I'll build something **special**,"

decided the **bear**,

"that **Rabbit** and **Squirrel**

and **Owl** can all share."

He thought, "I shall make something **bigger** than **BIG**: a towering heart made of **flowers** and twigs."

He **gathered**

some tree bark

and **branch bundles** too,

then stuck them together

with **honeycomb** glue.

Then he
**painted**
and **plaited**
and **knitted** and **weaved**

to **cover** the branches
in flowers and **leaves.**

"**Hurrah!**" cried out Ted,
once the **heart** was complete.
"It's the **tallest** of tall
and the **sweetest** of sweet!"

He tied it with **ribbon** and picked up the ends,
then **dragged** the big heart up the hill to his friends.

"I've made you a gift," cried the **sweet** little bear. "This **heart** is to show you all how much **I care**."

"It's **lovely**," gasped Owl.

"It's **BIG!**" Rabbit said.

And **shy** little Squirrel just **beamed** up at Ted.

"May I take it **first**?" hooted Owl to the rest.

"This heart will look **beautiful** up in my nest."

So he **pulled**
and he **pecked**
and he **tugged**
at the **gift**,

but the **flowery heart**
was **too heavy** to lift!

So Rabbit piped up,
"Let's give MY home a try!"
And the friends dragged the heart
to her burrow nearby.

But the heart was so big,
and the burrow so small,

that the friends couldn't
push the heart
down there at all.

So **shy** little Squirrel squeaked, "What about me? Perhaps it will **fit** in my **hole** in the tree."

But the hollow had **hundreds**
of acorns inside –

*there just* **wasn't room**
*for a heart of that* **size!**

Poor Ted cried, "It's hopeless! The heart is too tall. This gift that I've made is of no use at all."

But Owl said, "Don't worry," and gave Ted a hug.

"The real gift is knowing your heart's full of love."

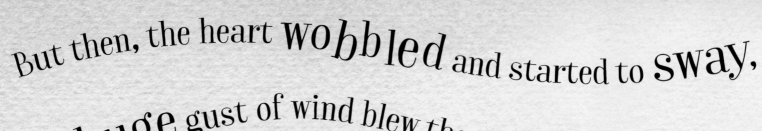

But then, the heart **wobbled** and started to **sway,**
as a **huge** gust of wind blew the whole thing away.

"**Oh, no!**" cried out Ted,
and he started to dash

as they **heard** in the **distance . . .**

a heart-breaking

# CRASH!

But then Ted got closer, and –

could it be true?

The broken-off pieces

were all heart-shaped too.

"They're perfect," cried Ted
as he gathered them all.
"There are some for each friend,
and they're lovely and small."

His friends were **delighted**,

and thanked the young bear.

And soon **all** their houses

had hearts **everywhere**.

So Ted learnt that sometimes
the best gifts of all
could be lovely and thoughtful
without being TALL!

THE END